# FINDING ANNABEL

# FINDING ANNABEL

*by*

ADÈLE GERAS

*Illustrated by Alan Marks*

HAMISH HAMILTON
LONDON

*For Norm . . . whose idea it was*

*First published in Great Britain 1987 by*
*Hamish Hamilton Children's Books*
*27 Wrights Lane, London W8 5TZ*
*Copyright © 1987 by Adèle Geras*
*Illustrations copyright © 1987 by Alan Marks*

British Library Cataloguing in Publication Data
Geras, Adèle
    Finding Annabel.—(Antelope)
    I. Title    II. Marks, Alan

ISBN 0-241-12302-X

Filmset in Baskerville by
Katerprint Typesetting Services, Oxford
Printed in Great Britain at the
University Press, Cambridge

## Chapter 1

"IS THIS SEAT taken, dear?"

Kaye glanced up from the book she was reading and saw that the lady who had spoken to her looked like somebody's grandmother.

"No, nobody's sitting there," she said and smiled as the lady squeezed herself with some difficulty between the seat and the edge of the table, and put a large wicker basket down in front of her.

"There," she said, "that's better. Now I'll just get my knitting out and then we can have a chat. I find that chats make journeys simply fly by, don't you?"

"Well," Kaye said, rather hesitantly. The old lady chuckled.

"Oh, I know what you've been told: never talk to strangers and quite right too, in this day and age, but me — well, I couldn't be more harmless if I tried."

Of course, Kaye thought, if she *was* a kidnapper or a murderer, she wouldn't exactly tell me the minute she saw me, would she? And anyway, Dad told the guard to look after me, all the way to Pensthorpe so she couldn't try anything even if she wanted to . . .

"I expect," said the old lady, "your mother's told the guard to keep an eye on you, hasn't she?"

"I haven't got a mother," said Kaye. "She died when I was born. I never even saw her. Her name was Annabel."

"Oh my stars," said the lady, her knitting-needles suddenly silent. "Oh, I am sorry. That's very sad for you.

Still," (the needles began their whispery clicking again), "I expect your father looks after you. Gives you a double share of love, like. Yours and your mother's."

"Yes, but," Kaye found she couldn't go on because her throat was suddenly clogged with tears.

"I expect, though," said the lady, "he'll be wanting to get married again, won't he?"

"How did you know?" Kaye was amazed.

"It's quite the normal thing, dear, and I put two and two together seeing your face. It clouded over like an April sky before a shower. Don't you like her, then, your father's fiancée? Is that it?"

"No, no, it isn't that. I mean I do like her," Kaye said. "Well, in a way I do. She's called Dulcie. She's quite pretty

4

and she wears nice clothes, and she always smells of flowers and brings me books and records whenever she visits. Sometimes I think she's just pretending to like me so that Dad will be happy. And she's very fussy and clears plates away before you've even swallowed your food, and sometimes she tells me off and the very worst thing about her is . . . " Kaye paused. She hadn't spoken to anyone in this way for ages, especially not someone she'd never met before.

"Just wait one second," said the lady, "while I count these stitches here. Ninety, ninety-two, ninety-four . . . that's better . . . go on . . . You were telling me what the very worst thing about her is . . . "

"Her son Nicky. He's six. He's horrible. He breaks things and tells tales and never wants to be out when we play cricket. And now he's going to live with us . . . " Kaye's eyes filled with tears. "I don't know what I'll do . . . "

"He won't always be six, though, will he? Stands to reason. How old are you?"

"I'm nine. Ten in September."

"Just picture yourselves when you're twenty-five and twenty-two. There won't be a smidge of difference between you then. Wait and see."

"But that means you think he'll get better as he gets older, and you don't know that he will. He might stay horrible. He could even get more horrible. He could end up being the most horrible person in the world, couldn't he?"

"I suppose so," said the lady, "but I don't expect he will, not really. What I expect is, you'll get used to each other."

6

The needles clicked and the train wheels clicked and Kaye stared out of the window. It's funny, she thought, it's as if we're standing still and the countryside is flying along beside the train. Sheep — whoosh — gone, trees — whoosh — gone, hedges — whoosh — gone. Looking at it stopped Kaye from thinking, so she turned away and stared down at her book without seeing it properly. She was supposed, over the years, to have got used to not having a mother. After all, people said, it's not as if you've ever had one, so that you know what you're missing. Every day at the

end of school, seeing them all on the other side of the playground, all the mothers, Kaye felt a small pain somewhere where she couldn't reach it . . . and now Dulcie would stand there in her high-heeled shoes and her blue sheepskin coat, and kiss her every day, more loving than any ordinary mother, so that everyone would think how good she was, and not a bit like Snow White's stepmother in the story.

"Are you going to Easthaven?" the

lady said. "That's where I'm getting off."

"No, I'm going to Pensthorpe. I always go, every summer, just for a bit. I'm staying with my mother's aunt and uncle. She's called Lilian Grant, and he's called Edward Grant, but everybody calls him Granty. He's Lilian's brother. Lilian doesn't like being called Aunt or Great-Aunt. She says it makes her feel old, but I don't know why she minds. They're both quite old, really."

"That sounds lovely, dear. It's beautiful country round Pensthorpe. It must make a nice change for you, after the city."

"I like the city," Kaye said, thinking of the comforting traffic noises outside her bedroom window at home. At Stone House, the nights were silent, except for the occasional cry of an animal, and there were no street lights. Sometimes a bit of moonlight crept in — a feeble, greenish light which made the shadows in the corners, beside the chest of drawers and around the cupboard seem as black and endless as dark water. "But I like the country too, of course."

"I'd better pack up now dear," the lady smiled. "We'll be at Easthaven in about two minutes. You can come and visit me there, if you ever come to town. I've got a wool shop on Albion Street.

Clarrie's Wools. That's the name." As
she spoke, she was rolling her knitting
wool up tidily, packing it into the
wicker basket, smoothing down her
hair, and finally she stood up.

"It's been a pleasure to speak to you,
young lady. I'm afraid I don't know
your name."

"Kaye Allen."

"Very nice, I'm sure. I hope we see
each other again. Come and visit me at

Clarrie's Wools." She made her way slowly up the compartment towards the door and waved as the train slowed down. Kaye waved back. As Easthaven slipped past the windows, Kaye picked up her book again. It was only fifteen minutes to Pensthorpe. Soon, she would see Granty and Lilian and Stone House. Soon, she would find out who had bought the cottage across the back field. Please, she thought, please let it be someone nice. She closed her eyes to wish hard, and when she opened them again, she saw that there was a very shiny silver camera lying on the seat that the lady (was her name Clarrie, like the shop?) had just left. It must be hers, Kaye thought, and reached over to pick it up. It didn't look like the kind of thing Clarrie would have had in her knitting-basket, but, Kaye thought, it must be hers. No one else has sat in that seat. Still, at least I know where I can give it back. I'll ask Lilian when I see her.

Kaye examined the camera carefully. That was the tiny window you looked through, and that was the button you pressed. A number at the bottom of a little hole said '17'. That was probably to tell you how many photographs had already been taken. The train, annoyingly, had stopped in the middle of an extremely boring empty field. Nothing to see at all except sheets of

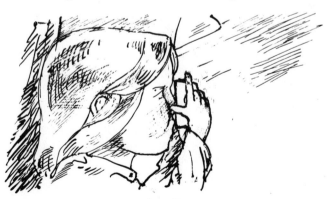

grass like green water stretching for miles. Kaye held the camera up to her eye and looked through the viewfinder at the field outside. Suddenly before she really knew what was happening, her finger seemed to find the button on its own and press. Kaye jumped. Whatever would Clarrie say? Wasn't it naughty to take pictures on other people's cameras? I'll have to buy her a new film, Kaye thought, and then she nearly dropped the camera in alarm. It had begun to buzz and whirr. It vibrated between her hands, and then something began to slide out of a slit in the bottom that Kaye hadn't noticed before. It's only a photo, Kaye thought. What a relief! It's one of those cameras that spits out the picture at once. Kaye held the photograph as the colours darkened into a copy of real colours, and thought, that's not right. There must be some mistake. I didn't take a picture like that ... there was only grass outside, I know there was. How could I possibly have taken a photo of a train? A train hasn't gone past the window, and even if one *had*, it wouldn't have been one like this, with a long smoke-scarf trailing in the sky behind it, clear as clear. There aren't any steam trains any more, are there?

Kaye shook her head, not knowing what to think. Perhaps she should ask someone. There was the guard, coming towards her.

"Nearly there now, miss," he said, stopping by Kaye's seat. "Better get your things together now." He took her suitcase down from the rack.

"Thank you," said Kaye. "Please, can you tell me if there are any steam trains that run on this line? Like this?" She held out the photograph for the guard to see. He peered down at it. "That . . . oh, she's the Whitecliffs to Victoria express, she is. I remember her, all right. Stopped running, oh, about thirty years ago, give or take a year or two. That's a remarkable picture now. Very clear, for such an old picture. Where did you get that?"

"Oh, I found it," said Kaye, thrusting it between the pages of her book. "Thanks very much for looking after me." She opened her case and buried the camera under a nightie.

At Pensthorpe, Kaye opened the door, jumped on to the platform and looked around the small station for Lilian. The train beside her started up again, and began to chug away. Suddenly a head leaned out of one of the windows, an arm waved and a voice began to shout at her. It was the guard.

"It's not possible," he was shouting. "They didn't have colour photos back then, did they? It's impossible." His voice grew fainter and finally disappeared in the clicking of the wheels as the train gathered speed and twisted out of sight.

"There you are, Kaye my lovey," said a voice, and Lilian was flapping up

18

the platform towards her, scarves flying, sleeves floating, trying to talk and get her breath back at the same time. "Come along now, the chariot awaits!"

Lilian always said that, every single year. Nothing ever changed at Pensthorpe. That was the main reason Kaye liked it. The three long strands of pearls around her great-aunt's neck were always there, swinging from side to side as she walked.

"Do you always wear them, Lilian, the pearls?" Kaye asked now as they walked towards the car park.

"Oh, always, child, always." Lilian chuckled. "Well, you never know who you're going to run into, do you, and you're always safe, my mama used to say, with chiffon and pearls. Come along now dear. Let's see if this old jalopy can make it to Stone House."

Kaye leaned back happily against the cracked leather seat, and said what she always said as the car left the station carpark, just as if she were repeating her part in a play: "Stone House, here we come!"

## Chapter 2

STONE HOUSE was beautiful. It was the only building for miles around, standing at the top of a small hill. At the back, fields began where the cottage garden ended, and across the fields stood the house which had been empty last year, but which this year Kaye hoped might contain someone to play with. In front of the house, there were flowerbeds and lawns sloping down to the road. On the other side of the road, the ground sloped up again and there were trees growing all the way up the hill, a forest of them, spreading out from the grey ribbon of the road to the pale milky sky, filling the whole window as the car passed by. In the middle of Stone House's front lawn stood Granty's greenhouse, with walls that looked like a patchwork quilt made up of different pieces of stained glass that Granty had put in over the years instead of the ordinary transparent kind.

"Anyone else," Lilian always said, "would put it round the back, out of sight, anywhere really, a bizarre old eyesore like that, not bang slap in the middle of the front lawn."

"But Granty loves it," Kaye said.

"Oh, I know dear. It's his pride and joy and all that." Lilian sighed. "I've tried to persuade him to move it, put a fountain in its place or something, but it's no good. He's an obstinate old thing, even if he is my brother. He potters around in there from morning till night . . . shouldn't be a bit surprised to hear him talking to the plants."

"Don't you ever go in there, Lilian?" Kaye had once asked.

"Me?" Lilian had looked genuinely astonished. "Never!" She leaned towards Kaye and lowered her voice. "Don't breathe a word, darling, but I can't abide the Great Outdoors. Give

me a theatre, a café, a lounge or a bedroom, even a kitchen at a pinch, and I'm as happy as a queen . . . but gardens, even gardens under glass, fields and woods . . . " she shivered elegantly. "I wouldn't really mind if I never saw another."

"Then why do you stay at Stone House?" Kaye wanted to know.

"Well, to look after Granty for one thing, and also because I can hardly go gallivanting around the world at my age, now can I?"

Kaye remembered those words now as Lilian parked the car. She took her case from the boot and walked over to the front steps, ready to go into the house.

"Have you said hello to the nymph?" Lilian called out. "Your mother, bless her, used to love that statue of the nymph . . . she used to say it reminded her of me . . . well, I'd say to her, I was a bit of a bobby-dazzler in my day, but never that fond of the water." She smiled at Kaye. "Come inside when you've had a good look."

The nymph was on a large, perfectly round plaque, just beside the front door. Her white and graceful figure stood out in high relief from a faded aquamarine background. Her hair and moulded draperies floated all around her, as though she had drifted up and up from the bottom of a clear pool. Best of all about the nymph, Kaye liked the fact that her mother had seen her too, and had thought she was lovely. But suddenly, looking at the statue, Kaye had a cold and terrifying thought. What if Lilian and Granty were to die? They were both old. She shivered. It wasn't only that she loved them both and would miss them, but also that when they died there would be no one left in the world who remembered Annabel as a child. Of course at home, Dad spoke about her mother, and there were albums full of photographs of a dark and pleasant-looking woman, but there were no pictures of the child Annabel. All the albums had been kept in a cellar at Stone House, and were destroyed one autumn night during a flood caused by collapsing drains. But Granty and

Lilian spoke often of Annabel as she was long ago, and when Kaye was most alone, she turned the stories over in her mind like a miser gloating over nuggets of gold.

Still, she thought, it's no good sitting out here being miserable. I must go and unpack. "Here I come, Lilian," she called out.

"Good girl," said Lilian from the kitchen. "Put your things away and then come and have some lunch."

Kaye always slept in the smallest

bedroom. ("Your mother," Lilian had said, "liked it best because she could see the greenhouse. She was almost as potty about that extravaganza as Edward . . . they used to go to auctions and come back chortling and rubbing their hands together over yet another piece of Victorian stained glass. Doleful maidens with hair like coils of rope and skinny flowers in puce and acid green . . . still, they were happy. They were going to turn it into a cathedral among greenhouses.")

She put her clothes into the chest of drawers, and then remembered the camera, and the mysterious steam train picture she had taken. Perhaps it would be better, she thought, not to say anything to Lilian. They'd be bound to visit Easthaven one day during the week. Lilian could never stay away from town for very long . . . and then she could give the camera back to Clarrie. The little number at the bottom of the hole said '18'. Well, Kaye thought, I've taken one picture already. I could take one of this room. It's sunny enough. I'll have to get a new film as it is, and it's such fun watching the photo slide out. Kaye pressed the button and waited for the whirring and the buzzing to stop. Now I'll have a souvenir of this room to take home with me and when life with Nicky gets too dreadful, then I'll take it out and look at it. But what's this? She frowned. The photograph looked nothing like this room. There were flowered curtains at the window for one thing. What had happened to the pink and white stripes that hung there now? And where was the window seat? There was a desk there, and not

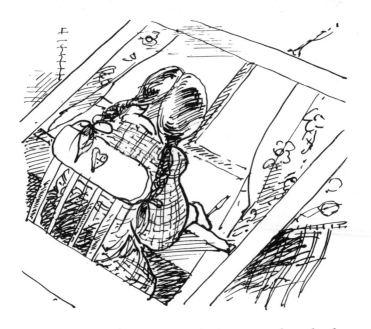

only that, someone sitting at the desk.
You could only see her back. She had
long dark plaits and was wearing a
tartan dress with very full, puffed-up
sleeves. Kaye felt cold all over. She put
the photograph down on the bed. She
took the picture of the steam train out
of the book and looked at it. This is
impossible, thought Kaye, and yet it's

happened. Twice This camera is taking photographs of things that were
there a long time ago. If I tell someone,
they might take the camera away. The
number says '19' now, so I've probably
only got five photographs left on the film.
She glanced at the picture of the girl's
back. Who would be sitting like that in
this room? Kaye had a shivery feeling
that she knew the answer, but how
could she check that it really was a
photograph of her mother without making Lilian suspicious? I've got it, she
thought. I'll ask Granty. He gets mixed
up all the time anyway and Lilian
hardly ever listens to him properly . . .
he'll tell me, and then forget about telling me the very next minute. I'll go
down before lunch and catch him in the
greenhouse. Who's this, I'll say, just
like that . . .

## Chapter 3

"WHO'S THIS?" said Granty. "Little Kaye, is it? Dear me. Is it really a year since last summer? How are you?"

"I'm very well, Granty. How are you? How are all the plants?"

"Ticking over . . . ticking over . . ." His thin body seemed thinner than ever, and as he nodded his head, he reminded Kaye of a dandelion clock: soft, grey tufts of hair, wispy enough to blow away in a strong wind. He shuffled along between wooden benches crowded with pots, stopping from time to time to touch the different kinds of leaves. There were striped leaves, speckled leaves, fringed leaves, velvet leaves, leaves with prickles, leaves with veins, ferny leaves, fleshy leaves, leaves of green and purple and blue and grey and nearly black, leaves as wide as dinner plates and as small as a thumb-nail, round leaves, long leaves, tapering leaves and plump leaves and hardly a flower to be seen among the whole lot of them.

"Not interested in flowers," Granty had muttered once. "Flowers come and go, my dear, but leaves go on for ever, near as dammit."

"Granty, can I show you some-thing?" Kaye said now.

"What's that, child? Something interesting, is it? You've got it tucked away behind your back . . . "

"It's a photograph."

34

"Let's have a look then." He reached out a hand that trembled a little. Kaye gave him the photograph. He held it up close to his face.

"That's Annabel," he said and handed it back to Kaye and shook his head. "I don't know where that came from, I'm sure. I thought Lilian said all the photos had gone in the flood . . . still, maybe not. She died, you know. Annabel, I mean."

"Yes, I know, Granty. She died when I was born. I'm her daughter. I'm Kaye."

"Of course you are. Silly of me. Kaye. Annabel was much darker than you. She had long, dark plaits. She found the Rose Window. Did I tell you?"

"No, tell me about it now," Kaye said, and sat down on a bench to listen.

She'd heard the story before, of course, but she didn't mind hearing it again. Kaye imagined all Granty's stories wound up in his head on a long cassette tape, and sometimes he'd tell one and sometimes another, and the same stories would come round over and over again, but it didn't matter.

"We called it the Rose Window," he said, "Annabel and I, as a kind of joke, do you see? They've got a magnificent Rose Window in Notre Dame in Paris ... very grand ... and when we found ... well, let's see. We were walking in Easthaven one day, Annabel and I. There was a tea-room on the Esplanade that gave one rainbow ice-creams: three colours in a silver dish and a wafer for good measure. Annabel always had ice-cream and I had scones and tea ... "

"And Lilian?" Kaye knew that she
had to ask questions from time to time
to keep the story flowing.

"Oh, Lilian was in and out of all the shops like a jack-in-the-box: milliners, dress shops, haberdashers, shoe shops . . . So Annabel and I took to wandering about. Now Easthaven, as you know, is a very respectable town, so you can imagine our surprise when we saw, in the middle of a perfectly well-kept row of houses, an extremely startling, not to say shocking sight . . . "

"And what was that?" Kaye asked.

"Why, a bona-fide, hundred-percent, sure-fire guaranteed, copper-bottomed haunted house!" Granty looked amazed all over again.

"'It's haunted, Granty,' Annabel said . . . she was the one who first called me that . . . Granty . . . She said : 'Let's go in and see what we can see'. The house was derelict. The doors hung open, the windows were broken, the

40

rooms, from the road where we stood, seemed cavernous and empty. The neatly-painted houses on either side of it seemed to have turned away, shrunk back into themselves, as if to say: we're good, proper, occupied houses. We're having nothing to do with you. I knew I ought to take Annabel away from there, but she was too quick for me. In a trice, she'd flown up the stairs and in at the front door. She was an impulsive child, and packed so full of curiosity that she quite forgot to be frightened, more often than not. I followed her in (to fetch her out) but she was already upstairs. 'Look what I've found, Granty . . . I knew we had to come in . . . treasure'. I went upstairs rather gingerly, I can tell you. Annabel was holding up a bed-room door that had fallen off its hinges. 'Isn't it lovely?' she said. 'Please let's take it home. Please, Granty. No one else wants it'. Well, she knew that stained glass was my weakness . . . and this door had a most wonderful panel at the top . . . there it is . . . over there . . . isn't it grand?"

Kaye looked up at the scarlet glass
rose. It stood in a pattern made by
curves of green and blue glass, bounded
with strips of gilded lead. Two blue
tulips stood beside the rose, one on
either side.

"Yes, it's lovely," Kaye said. "But she found something else as well, didn't she?"

"It was a silver locket . . . or maybe a ring or a bracelet. I can't quite recall. It was a long time ago."

"What happened to the locket?" Kaye wanted to know. Granty looked vague.

"Haven't the foggiest, my dear. Annabel put it in her pocket, and that's the last I saw of it . . . but the window. We carried the whole door out of there, and down the road with some difficulty, and Lilian's face when we told her we wanted to strap it to the roof-rack . . . well, it was a sight to see. I think it was worth it, though." Granty rubbed his nose thoughtfully. "Let me see . . . isn't it nearly lunchtime? We'd better potter back to the house."

44

Kaye followed Granty across the front lawn. She was thinking about the five photos she had left . . . Where could she point the camera and be sure of catching Annabel? She wished there was someone she could talk to.

As they reached the kitchen door, Lilian came out to meet them.

"Darlings, look who I've invited for lunch . . . it's Sally Thomas, the little girl from next door."

"Hello," said the girl who had slip-

46

ped out of the kitchen and was now standing beside Lilian, smiling. She was wearing jeans and a white T-shirt and looked very much like a small lion with a mane of thick sandy hair standing out like a frill around her face. Kaye liked the look of her immediately.

"I'm Kaye," she said.

"I know," said Sally. "I've been dying for you to arrive. There's no one to play with for miles and miles . . . "

As they walked into the kitchen,

Kaye decided, I'll tell Sally about the camera. Maybe she'll have a good idea, and even if she doesn't, she'd never tell a secret. You can see just by looking at her that she wouldn't.

## Chapter 4

THE THOMAS'S HOUSE was a mess. It was as though someone had taken tall, skinny Mrs Thomas and short, plump Mr Thomas, and Sally and her sister Wendy and her two brothers, Hugh and Roddy (Roddy was a baby) and stirred them up in a thick soup made of cups, plates, felt tips with the lids left off them, bits of Lego, drying nappies, cotton reels, pieces out of jigsaws, naked Sindy dolls, assorted hair ribbons, crusts left over from tea, yesterday's newspaper, odd socks, school exercise books, and a very glittery pink leotard.

49

"That's Wendy's," Sally said "She thinks she's going to be a dancer on T.V. She practises all day. Even when I'm trying to get to sleep at night. I think you're lucky, being on your own."

"And I think you're lucky. At least you've got your own brothers and sister. My new brother'll be a stranger really. And you've got a mother."

Sally frowned. "Don't see her much, though. She's too busy, usually, with the baby and the washing and the cooking and shopping and everything. She works ever so hard."

"Still, she is there when you want her. I've never even seen mine . . . I wonder about her all the time. I wonder what she was like when she was my age. Do you ever ask your mum things about when she was a girl?"

"No, I don't." Sally looked amazed

at the idea. "I've never thought of it. She talks about it sometimes, her school and everything, but I never listen."

"If I had a mother I'd listen to every word she said."

"Bet you wouldn't."

"Would."

"Wouldn't . . . oh, come on, let's stop all this. Let's do something exciting. Are you good at thinking of exciting things to do?"

"Not particularly. Only . . . well, I have got a secret. It's also a kind of treasure-hunt."

"Great! Are you going to tell me about it, or what?"

Kaye told Sally the whole story. She picked up the carrier bag she had brought with her and took out the camera and the photographs.

"Crumbs!" Sally said, after she had

looked for a long time. "It's weird. Aren't you scared?"

"No." Kaye looked worried. "I don't think photos can hurt you, can they?"

"It's a bit funny, though," said Sally. "How are you going to decide what to take photos of? Is it just your mother you're looking for? Is she the treasure? I wouldn't call that treasure."

"That's because your mother's in the kitchen, making lunch. You'd feel different if she wasn't there."

"I suppose so . . . but still, I don't call it real treasure."

"Then call it something else," Kaye said. "I don't care. We've got to decide on a plan, though. Some kind of plan, because we've only got today and tomorrow. The day after that, we're going to Easthaven, and then I'll have to return the camera."

55

"Well, in books they make lists. You know, 'Ten Likely Spots' or something. Do you know about her favourite places? Did she have a hideout or something? Or a treehouse?"

"I suppose," said Kaye, "we could start with the greenhouse. I know she liked that. I know that her room is the one I'm in . . . I know she liked the nymph . . . "

"That's a good start, then. That's three places already, and we've only got five pictures left. Let's go down to Stone House and begin now. It's dead exciting really."

"We'll have to eat lunch first, won't we? Your mum's getting it ready."

"Then we'll go straight after," Sally said.

After lunch the girls ran down to Stone House and began to prowl around the garden.

"Do you think the outside of the greenhouse," Sally asked "or the inside?"

"Inside," said Kaye, after thinking for a moment. "Now, while it's empty."

Granty was sleeping quietly in a deckchair under a tree on the other side of the lawn. The two girls went in and Sally closed the door carefully behind them.

"I know," said Kaye, "let's take a picture of the Rose Window. Annabel found it."

"Where is it?"

"There." Kaye pointed to where the light shone through the scarlet glass. "I'll take a picture of it . . . "

"Be careful, though," said Sally. "Look, if I stand here, the window is miles higher than my head. Your mother certainly wouldn't have been floating three feet off the ground."

"Right," said Kaye. "You stand there and I'll take a picture of you. Don't move."

"Don't be daft," Sally said. "It's not going to be of me, is it?"

"Don't know yet . . . look, it's starting, come and see. Here it is . . . oh, my goodness, she's here. Look Sally, . . . that's her. My . . . Annabel. Look, she's staring straight at us . . . she's holding something. Oh, Sally, it's almost as if . . ."

"Let me see," said Sally. "Please let me look . . . I can't believe it. In a minute we'll wake up. It's magic and it's so clear. You can see it's a picture of

in here . . . there's the edge of the window . . . there aren't half as many plants though. What is it she's holding, can you see?"

"Let me look . . . it's a chain of some kind . . . oh." Kaye stopped suddenly. "I bet I know what it is."

Kaye told Sally about the locket.

"I bet it's that. I bet it was a real jewel. I bet she never told anyone about it because it was so valuable. Granty said he never saw it again."

"She must have hidden it," Sally said. "That's what I'd do with treasure."

"But if it was valuable," Kaye said, "she wouldn't have left it hidden. She'd

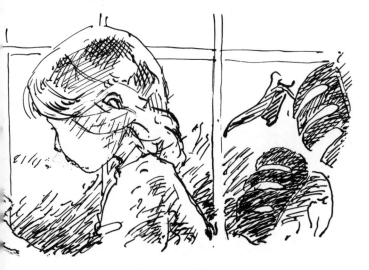

have come back when she was older and unhidden it. It's probably just lost."

"Anyway," Sally said, "we were lucky here, so we can try the bedroom now."

Kaye was still looking at the photograph. In this picture, you could see Annabel's face quite clearly.

"Do you think I look like her a bit?" she asked Sally. Sally considered.

"Not a bit," she said finally. "You must take after your dad."

For a split second Kaye felt like breaking one of Granty's plant-pots over Sally's head, but the moment passed. Kaye realized that Sally was telling the truth. I look, she thought, nothing at all like my mother. Everyone had always said she was a copy of her father, but Kaye had lived in hope. As long as there were no photographs of Annabel as a child, it was possible to imagine. Now, this pale, oval face with long dark plaits and a serious look about the eyes even when the mouth was smiling had put an end to Kaye's fantasies.

"Hello, Annabel," she said, under her breath.

65

"Are you talking to me?" Sally asked.

"No, just muttering. . . come on . . . let's go up to my room."

There was no sign of Annabel in the picture they took in the bedroom, nor of the locket either. There was only the desk, with a letter on it now, and an envelope.

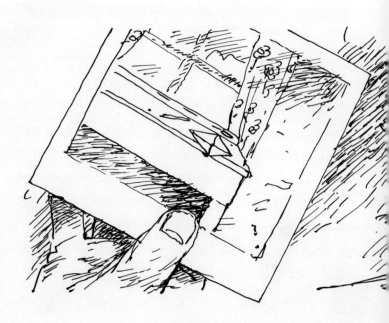

"Perhaps," said Sally, "the chest of drawers has hidden compartments. She could have put the locket in there. Let's take one of that."

The photograph that appeared showed someone just coming into the room.

"That's my Granny," said Kaye. "Annabel's mother. There's a picture of her in an album at home. It's no use at all."

"We've only got two pictures left,"
said Sally. "I think we should try outside again."

"The nymph!" Kaye said. "Lilian's often told me she loved the nymph. Come on."

The two girls went outside and stood on the front steps of Stone House looking at the blue plaque on the wall.

"You stand there," said Kaye and stepped back until she could see both Sally and the nymph in the viewfinder. When the picture slid out, they looked at it and there was Annabel again.

"We've done it!" shouted Kaye. "We've found her again."

"Yes," said Sally, "but that's all we've found isn't it? Where's the treasure? What happened to the locket?" Sally frowned. "I don't want to be mean or anything, seeing as it's your mum and you're seeing her for the first time and everything, but whatever is she doing? She looks really silly in this photo."

"I don't know," Kaye said quietly. She couldn't be angry with Sally because the truth was that Annabel *did* look a bit stupid. She was standing beside the nymph, smiling. She'd put one finger in front of her lips, as if she were telling the nymph to ssh! It must have been some silly game she'd been playing. Just my luck, thought Kaye, and only one photograph left.

"What shall we do with the last one?" Sally asked.

"I don't know . . . maybe another one of the nymph. Maybe it'll turn out better."

The last photograph (and the girls knew it was the last because no more numbers appeared at the bottom of the little hole after they'd taken it) was of a

70

younger Granty with thick, dark hair and a moustache fixing the plaque with the nymph on it to the wall. Of course it was interesting to see how different he looked, but still, Kaye felt vaguely disappointed.

"Cheer up," said Sally. "You've got three photos of your mum you never had before."

"I suppose so," Kaye said. "Thanks for helping me, anyway. I'm sorry there wasn't any treasure."

"You did say there might not be any . . . it's O.K. Anyway, I did like using a magic camera." Sally grinned. "I've got to go now. Come and tell me what happens in Easthaven when you get back. We're all going to Whitecliffs for the day tomorrow."

"O.K. 'Bye." Sally was gone, through the garden and running across the back field towards the cottage. Kaye took the camera and the photographs back to her bedroom. She spread the Annabel pictures on the bed. Annabel writing. Annabel holding something in the greenhouse. Annabel looking stupid, telling the nymph to ssh! Such a pity about the photo of the empty desk . . . it really did look as if

Annabel had just pushed back her chair and gone . . . where? Perhaps, thought Kaye, she went to get the locket . . .

"Kaye dear," Lilian's voice came to her from far away. "Tea time."

"I'm coming," Kaye called back, and put the camera carefully into her bag, ready to take back to Clarrie's Wools. The photographs she put back in her book. Sally was right. Having the pictures of Annabel should be treasure enough. Still, a nagging thought at the back of Kaye's mind kept insisting that there was something else.

## *Chapter 5*

"SO THEN WHAT HAPPENED?" asked Sally. The girls were sitting on the front steps of Stone House.

"Nothing really. I don't know what I'd been expecting," said Kaye, "but it was a bit boring. I bought a film at Boots and then we found the wool shop and there was Clarrie, and she was ever so pleased and thanked me and gave me a kiss . . . said she'd missed her camera and how good I was to give it back, and that was it."

"Oh, well," said Sally. "Never mind."

"But I'll tell you another thing," said Kaye, "and that's that the camera isn't magic at all. It was the film. It must have been. The camera was perfectly normal."

"How do you know?"

"Because Clarrie put the new film in, right there in the shop and she made Lilian take a picture with it of her and me together. Look." Kaye held out a snapshot of herself and an elderly lady standing in front of a pyramid of balls of wool.

"That's you, all right," said Sally, and sighed. "I wonder where Clarrie bought the magic film?" She stood up and looked at the nymph. "I also wonder," she said, "why your mum was telling this nymph to keep quiet. What kind of game was it?"

"Perhaps she was telling her to keep a secret," Kaye said.

"Like where she'd hidden the locket?"

Kaye's eyes shone with excitement. "Of course! She hid it under the plaque . . . we've even got a photo of Granty putting it up. I bet there's a space in the wall behind it, and she put the locket in there . . . "

"But that means we'll never get it out, not without taking the whole thing off the wall, and we can't do that by ourselves . . . we'd have to ask Lilian or Granty and then they'd have to know everything."

Kaye thought for a moment. "Perhaps there's a sliding bit, or a brick that comes out or something . . . let's just have a look."

She prodded all the bricks around the plaque. Nothing moved. Then she began to touch the nymph herself, pressing the carved edges of the circle. To her surprise, as she pushed it, the whole plaque moved slightly on the wall.

"It's not fixed on at all," Sally shouted. "Look, it must be hung up on a giant nail, like a picture. Do you think we can lift it off?"

"Let's try," said Kaye. Together, they pushed and pulled and strained and at last, the nymph came off the wall, pulling with it the nail it had been hanging on. The girls, staggering under the weight, lowered the plaque as carefully as they could to the ground.

"I can feel paper," Sally said. "It's stuck to the back of this thing. And

something lumpy, all wrapped up. I bet
that's the locket."

"Let's see." Kaye looked at the
underside of the nymph as Sally held it
a little way off the ground. "Gosh,
there's something wedged into the back
of the frame . . . it's . . . " Kaye brought
out a pink envelope. "It looks like
the envelope in the photograph . . . I

82

think . . . I think it's from her . . . from Annabel," she whispered. "And there's something in it . . . it's a letter to someone . . . perhaps it's the same letter that was on her desk . . . "

"Aren't you going to read it?"

"Yes, yes I will . . . The date says August 25th, 1956.

'Dear Frances,

Thank you very much for having me to stay last week. I thought your house was jolly nice. Of course I never saw it when your mother was still alive, so I have to take your word for it that it was even better then. I don't think your stepmother is awful, actually. I expect you'll get to like her in the end, and not be like Cinderella at all. At the station, while you were getting platform tickets, she told me she liked having you for a daughter, only she felt a bit shy about telling you, so there. I agree about Bobby. He is a pest, but he's very little, so perhaps he'll be better when he grows up. He'll probably go away to school, anyway. In any case, he's someone. It's better than being on your own. My mother says can you come and stay next hols? Ask for permission *now*.

See you next term.

Love,

Annabel.

84

P.S. I found a locket in a haunted house. I think it's silver but Granty says it's from a Christmas cracker. If you wear it, it turns your neck black. I've put in a picture of me and you. Just our heads, cut out.'"

"Unwrap this," said Sally. "Let's have a look." They took the paper off the locket and opened it. The picture had cracked and faded, but there was Annabel, her head very close to someone with yellow, curly hair.

"That must be Frances," said Kaye, "her friend."

Kaye looked down at the letter. Why had Annabel never sent it to her friend? Why had she hidden it here? It was almost as though she meant Kaye to find it. She felt, because Frances, too, had a stepmother, as though Annabel had written to *her*. That was silly. She wasn't a mother then, just Annabel. But maybe Dulcie is shy too, like

Frances' stepmother, Kaye thought. Maybe it'll be hard for her, getting a new daughter. Now that I have this letter and the pictures and the locket, I feel I know Annabel a little ... Whenever I need to, I can look at all these things, and they'll be like a message straight from my mother to me ... and I can ask Sally to come and stay with me sometimes, too. In the holidays, just like Annabel did ...

Kaye turned to Sally.

"Let's go and find Granty," she said, "and tell him that the nymph fell off the wall."